P9-AOW-849

For Mandy
J. C.

For Hayley and Bump
M. H.

Text copyright © 2020 by John Condon · Illustrations copyright © 2020 by Matt Hunt · Nosy Crow and its logos are trademarks of Nosy Crow Ltd.
Used under license. · All rights reserved. No part of this book may be reproduced, transmitted, or stored in an information retrieval system in any form
or by any means, graphic, electronic, or mechanical, including photocopying, taping, and recording, without prior written permission from the publisher.
First U.S. edition 2020 · Library of Congress Catalog Card Number pending · ISBN 978-1-5362-1216-7
This book was typeset in Tropen. · The illustrations were done in mixed media.
Nosy Crow, an imprint of Candlewick Press, 99 Dover Street, Somerville, Massachusetts 02144 · www.nosycrow.com · www.candlewick.com
20 21 22 23 24 25 APS 10 9 8 7 6 5 4 3 2 1 · Printed in Humen, Dongguan, China

JOHN
CONDON

ILLUSTRATED BY
MATT
HUNT

# THE PIRATES ~ARE~ COMING!

ST. JOHN THE BAPTIST PARISH LIBRARY
2920 NEW HIGHWAY 51
LAPLACE, LOUISIANA 70068

nosy crow
An imprint of Candlewick Press

Every day, Tom climbed
the hill to watch for pirates.

It had been a long time
since anyone had seen them,
but Tom knew they would be back.

So he waited . . .
and waited . . .
and waited
until at last he saw . . .

a ship!

And quick as a flash, everybody hid.

CLOSED

DING!

DING!

They waited . . .                    and waited . . .

and waited          UNTIL . . .

it was clear there were NO pirates, just a little fishing boat bobbing home.

"Tom," said the villagers, "that's not even a ship."

"That's OK, Tom," said his dad. "Just remember, pirate ships are BIG."

Tom knew it was very important to keep watching, and so the next day, he went back up the hill.

And again he waited . . .

and waited . . .

and waited

until at last he saw . . .

a ship!

A **big** ship.

And once again, everybody hid.

They waited . . .

and waited . . .

and waited

UNTIL . . .

it was very clear there were STILL no pirates,
just a rusty old steamboat chugging back to shore.

"Tom," said the villagers, "that's
the slowest ship we've ever seen!"

"That's OK, Tom," said his dad.
"Just remember, pirate ships are
big and fast."

Tom knew someone had to keep watching, and so the next day, he went back up the hill. And again he waited . . .

and waited . . .

and waited

until at last he saw . . .

a ship! A big ship.

A big, fast ship.

DING!

DING!

"PIRATES!"

shouted Tom.

"THE PIRATES ARE COMING! THE PIRATES ARE COMING! QUICK! EVERYBODY HIDE!"

And once again (but not quite as quickly this time), everybody hid.

They waited . . . and waited . . . and waited UNTIL . . .

it was very clear there were definitely NO pirates, just a
big merchant ship pulling into the dock.

"TOM!" said the villagers.
"That is NOT a pirate ship!"

"That's OK, Tom," said his dad
gently. "Just remember, pirate
ships are big and fast, and they
have a special pirate flag."

When Tom trudged up the hill the next day,
he brought his favorite book, some crayons,
and his teddy bear, and got ready for a long wait.

But suddenly . . .

he saw a ship.

A **big** ship.

A **big**, **fast** ship.

A BIG, FAST ship with
a SPECIAL PIRATE FLAG!

# "PIRAAA

yelled Tom, running into the village.

But

nobody hid.

Not even Dad.

DING!

DING!

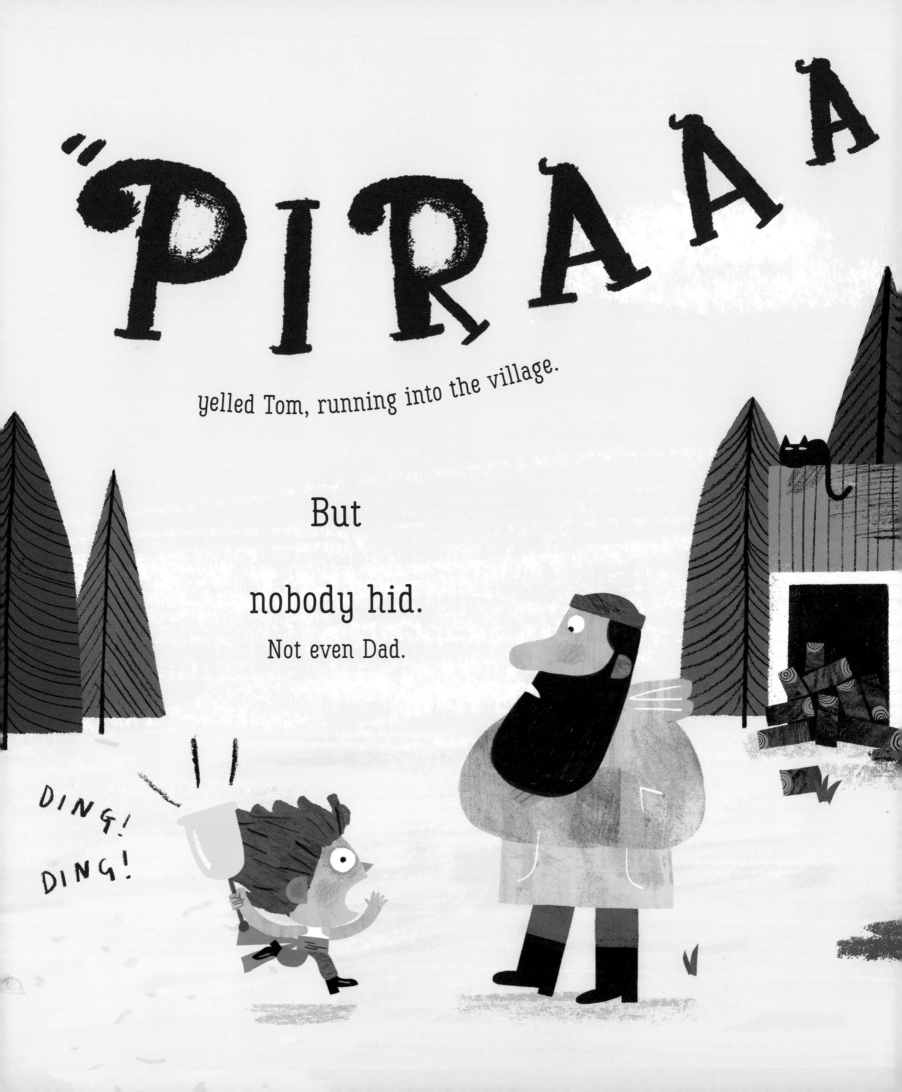

ST. JOHN PARISH LIBRARY

Meanwhile, the pirate ship sailed silently into the harbor. The gangplank fell with a *thud*, and the pirate captain ran ashore, with the pirate crew close behind.

Nobody heard the pirates as they climbed the steps to the village. Nobody heard them as they made their way down the narrow streets. Until . . .

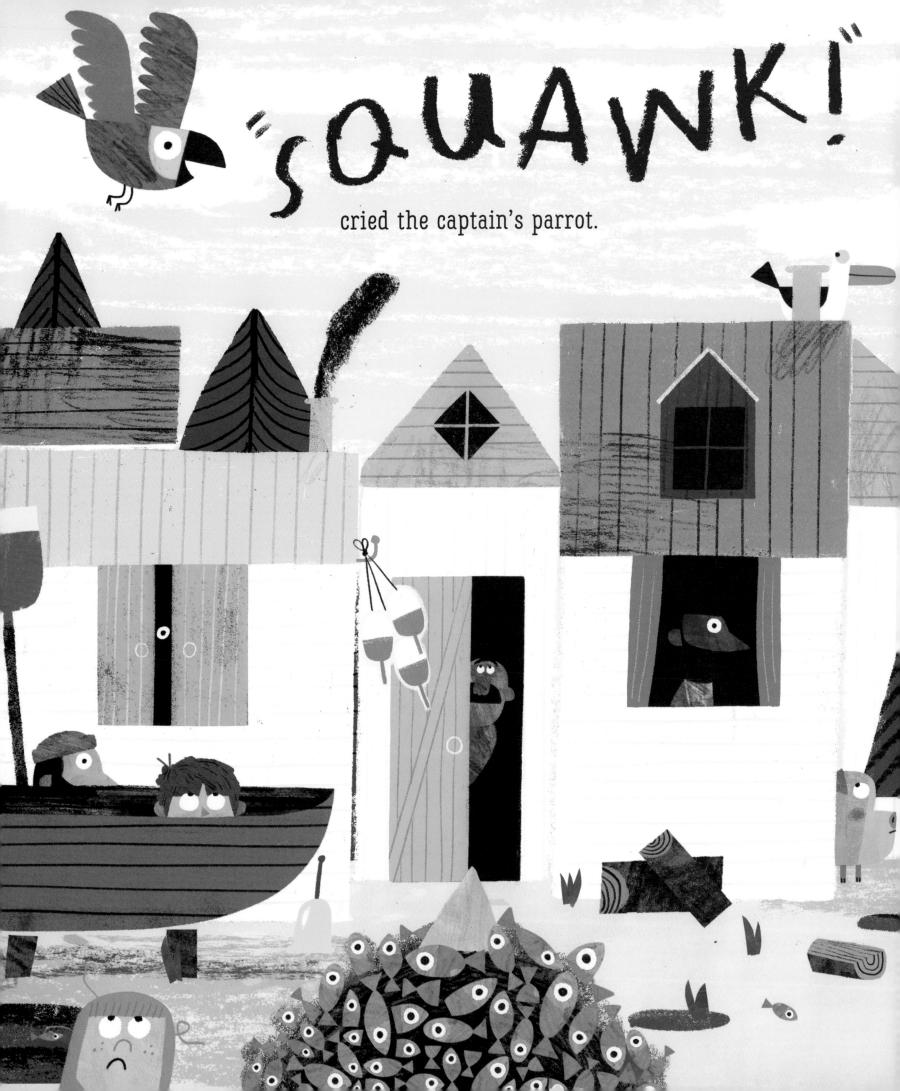

**"SQUAWK!"**
cried the captain's parrot.

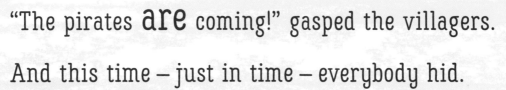

"The pirates **are** coming!" gasped the villagers.

And this time – just in time – everybody hid.

Moments later, the pirates marched
into the square.

"Where is everybody?" growled the
pirate captain.

Then
suddenly . . .

R I S E!" shouted the villagers. "Welcome home!"

"I missed you, Son!"
said the pirate captain.

"I missed you
more!" said Tom.

"Welcome home, Mom!"